Libby
the Writing
Fairy

Special thanks to Narinder Dhami

ISBN 978-0-545-70834-0

12 11 10 9 8 7 6 5 4 3 2 1   15 16 17 18 19 20/0

Printed in the U.S.A.   40

This edition first printing, March 2015

Libby
the Writing Fairy

by Daisy Meadows

SCHOLASTIC INC.

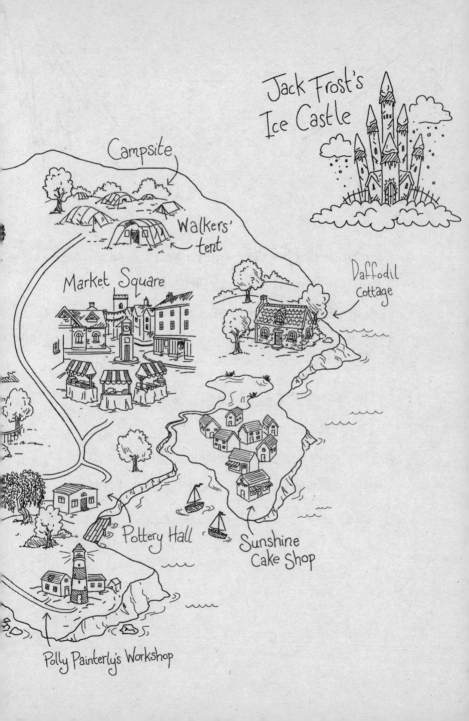

Jack Frost's
Ice Castle

Campsite

Walkers'
tent

Daffodil
Cottage

Market Square

Pottery Hall

Sunshine
Cake Shop

Polly Painterly's Workshop

I'm a wonderful painter — have you heard of me?
Behold my artistic ability!
With palette, brush, and paints in hand,
I'll be the most famous artist in all the land!

The Magical Crafts Fairies can't stop me!
I'll steal their magic, and then you'll see
That everyone, no matter what the cost,
Will want a painting done by Jack Frost!

Contents

scattered stories

"I wish I could paint like you, Kirsty!" Rachel Walker said, holding up her friend's picture to admire it. The two girls had gone to a painting workshop at Rainspell Lighthouse the day before. "Mom, don't you think this painting is really good?"

Mrs. Walker was sitting in a chair outside their tent, soaking up the sunshine. She smiled and nodded. "You're very talented, Kirsty," Mrs. Walker declared, holding up the canvas to take a closer look. "You got Rachel's hair and eye color exactly right, and that rainbow arching over her head looks beautiful."

"Thanks!" Kirsty Tate laughed. "Artie Johnson, the Crafts Week organizer, told me I should enter it in the competition tomorrow."

"And she also said you needed to

choose a title for it," Rachel reminded her.

"How about *Rachel Under a Rainbow*?" suggested Mr. Walker. He was also seated outside the tent, reading a book. "Perfect!" said Kirsty, and Rachel grinned. The girls were spending spring break on Rainspell Island with their parents, and they were having the best time ever! It was Crafts Week on Rainspell, so every day there were different activities for the girls to try. The Tates were staying at a b and b in the village, while the Walkers had rented a large tent on the campground. Rachel and Kirsty were taking turns spending one night at the b and b, and then the next at the campsite.

"Whenever I look at your painting, it reminds me of when we met the Rainbow Fairies right here on Rainspell Island, Kirsty," Rachel whispered.

"Me, too," Kirsty whispered back. "I'll never forget our first fairy adventure!"

"Girls, are you going to a Crafts Week workshop today?" called Mrs. Walker.

"Yes, Mom, but we haven't decided which one yet," Rachel replied.

"I think there might be a writing workshop this morning," Kirsty said. "One of the other kids in the painting class mentioned it yesterday."

"Maybe we could write a story about the Rainbow Fairies and take it to the workshop," Rachel whispered. "No one would ever guess it was true!"

"Great idea," Kirsty agreed.

The girls sat on the grass with pens and paper and began to scribble down their ideas.

"It all started when we both came to Rainspell Island on vacation and met on the boat," Rachel murmured.

"I thought we met in the village," Kirsty said, frowning.

Rachel thought for a minute and shook

her head. "No, I don't think so," she replied. "Then we rescued Fern the Green Fairy from the pot of gold."

"But we saw the rainbow first," Kirsty reminded her.

Rachel felt confused. "Did we?" she asked. "I don't remember that."

"Wasn't it Ruby the Red Fairy we rescued from the pot?" Kirsty wondered. "Or was it Sunny the Yellow Fairy?"

The girls stared doubtfully at each other. Suddenly, Mr. Walker groaned in disgust and threw down his book.

"This story doesn't make sense!" He sighed. "It's about a cowboy in the Wild West and it was great so far, really exciting. But now the cowboy just took off in a spaceship. How ridiculous!"

"Oh!" Kirsty's eyes grew round. "Rachel, I know why the stories are all going wrong. It's because of Jack Frost!"

When Rachel and Kirsty had arrived on Rainspell Island, they'd been greeted by Kayla the Pottery Fairy, one of the seven Magical Crafts Fairies. Kayla had explained that not only was it Crafts Week on Rainspell Island—it was Crafts Week in Fairyland, too! She'd invited the girls to join them for the opening ceremony of this very special occasion. All of the fairies were excited because King Oberon and Queen Titania would be choosing the very best crafts to display in their royal palace.

But as Rachel and Kirsty watched Queen Titania give her opening speech, Jack Frost and his goblins had appeared. They tossed paint-filled balloons into the horrified crowd! The Magical Crafts Fairies and Queen Titania herself had all been splattered with bright green paint, and in the chaos, Jack Frost and his goblins had stolen the Magical Crafts Fairies' special objects. What a mess!

"I am the best artist ever—no one else is allowed to be better than me!" Jack Frost had declared. Then, with one flick of his wand, he'd created a magic ice bolt that swept him and his goblins away to the human world—along with the magic objects. With the help of the

Magical Crafts Fairies, Kirsty and Rachel had agreed to track down as many of the special objects as they could. Both girls were determined to make sure that crafts in the human and fairy worlds would still be fun, instead of being ruined forever by Jack Frost's selfish behavior.

"Yes, Libby the Writing Fairy's magic object is still missing," Rachel murmured. "That's why our stories are all jumbled!"

Kirsty bit her lip anxiously. "Rachel, wouldn't it be terrible if stories everywhere were mixed-up messes?" she cried. "We'd never be able to read our favorite books again!"

"I know." Rachel sighed. "Jack Frost has really done it this time!"

"Let's look at the Crafts Week pamphlet and find out more about the writing workshop," suggested Kirsty.

The girls dashed into the tent and found the pamphlet. Rachel flipped through it.

"Here it is," she announced. "*Writing workshop in the park, led by best-selling children's author Poppy Fields.*"

"Poppy Fields!" Kirsty exclaimed,

thrilled. "She's one of our favorite writers!"

"I know!" Rachel agreed with a huge smile. "She's amazing. I *love* the way she retells old fairytales. I have all her books."

"Me, too," said Kirsty, grinning from ear to ear. "Let's head over to the park now. Maybe Poppy Fields will be able to help us with our story!"

Fairytale Fiasco!

The girls hurried off to the park in the village. When they arrived, they followed the signs and saw a group of kids seated on picnic blankets near the playground, waiting for the writing workshop to start. A dark-haired woman was perched on a beanbag chair in front of them, a pile of books by her side.

"Look, Kirsty," Rachel whispered excitedly as they found a place to sit. "That's Poppy Fields—I recognize her from the picture on her books!"

Kirsty and Rachel were both thrilled when Poppy grinned at them. "Welcome, girls," she called. "You're just in time. Hello, everyone, and welcome to my workshop!"

"Hello, Poppy," the group chorused.

"I know you're all here because you love stories," Poppy went on. "And so do I! I thought I'd start our workshop by reading a couple of my very own stories to you." She chose a book from the pile and opened it. "This is the story of Sleeping Beauty. Once upon a time, many years ago . . ."

Rachel and Kirsty settled down to listen. But it soon became clear that the story of Sleeping Beauty was completely wrong and *very* mixed-up! Princess Aurora pricked her finger on a knitting needle, not a spinning wheel, and she was only asleep for five years, not a hundred. Then, when the handsome prince woke Sleeping Beauty with a kiss, she yawned and went back to sleep! All of the kids laughed. Poppy, who'd been looking more and more confused as she read, quickly closed the book.

"Let's try another one," she suggested, picking up *Little Red Riding Hood*. But only two pages in, as Little Red Riding Hood walked through the woods to her grandmother's house, the wolf pounced on her and gobbled her up. That was the end of the story! Poppy looked shocked and the girls glanced sideways at each other.

"Poor Poppy," Rachel whispered. "She

doesn't know why all her stories are going so wrong."

"But *we* do," Kirsty replied in a low voice. "This is all because Jack Frost's goblins stole Libby the Writing Fairy's magic object!"

"I think someone's playing a joke on me," Poppy murmured, shaking her head. She forced a smile. "OK, everyone, why don't we write a new story together? That'll be fun! Can anyone think of a character we should write about?"

Everyone was silent. The girls racked their brains, but they couldn't think of a single idea.

"We could write about the park," a boy in the front row suggested.

"The park can be the setting for the story," Poppy explained gently, "but we need a *character*, someone who does something interesting."

This time, there was an even longer silence. Then a squirrel scampered past, tail waving.

"Our character could be a squirrel," Poppy said. "What do you think? Does anyone have any plot ideas?"

"The squirrel could run up a tree," Rachel offered hesitantly.

"Good start," Poppy replied. "Why does the squirrel climb the tree? Is he looking for something?"

Everyone stared blankly at Poppy.

"My brain won't work!" Kirsty muttered, frustrated.

"He could be looking for another squirrel, I guess," Poppy said with a shrug. "But that's not very exciting, is it?"

No one had anything to say—and Poppy seemed to be out of ideas, too! The girls could see that the writing workshop was getting worse and worse. They had to do something!

"How about you try writing your own stories?" Poppy said at last. She began handing out pretty notebooks with painted covers. "Then you can read them out loud to one another when you're done." She gave Kirsty a pink notebook decorated with daisies, and Rachel got a blue one with a golden sun on the front.

"I can't think of a single thing to write!" Rachel sighed. She put her notebook down on the rug and began digging through her backpack for her pencil case. "This is going to be the most boring story ever!"

Kirsty pulled a pen from her pocket and began scribbling down what they'd just said about the squirrel. But then she spotted a faint glow hovering around Rachel's notebook. Kirsty looked closely at it, confused. It almost seemed like the painted sun was glowing with a magical golden light.

"Look, Rachel—fairy magic!" Kirsty whispered, nodding at the notebook.

Quivering with excitement, but trying not to show it, the girls moved to the edge of the picnic blanket where no one else was sitting. Carefully, Rachel opened her notebook. A cloud of shimmering sparkles tumbled out, followed by a tiny fairy!

Super Scribe

"Remember me?" the fairy whispered in her sweet little voice, flicking rippling waves of golden hair out of her eyes. She was barefoot and wore a flowy, sea-green dress sparkling with silver stars. "I'm Libby the Writing Fairy."

"Libby, you're just in time," Kirsty told

her. "Our writing workshop is a total disaster!"

"We can't think of a single idea," Rachel added.

Libby frowned. "How terrible!" She sighed, then landed lightly on the blanket, staying out of sight behind Rachel and Kirsty. "I knew this was going to happen when Jack Frost stole my magic notebook. We can't let him win, girls! What would our human and fairy worlds be like without stories?"

"Terrible!" the girls said together.

"I love good stories," Libby continued, "but stories will never turn out right again unless I find my magic notebook! Will you help me?"

Rachel and Kirsty nodded eagerly.

"We love stories, too," Rachel told the little fairy. "But I don't think there will be many good ones written here today!" She glanced around at the rest of the group. Everyone was staring blankly at their notebooks. Libby and the girls could see that they'd hardly written anything! Poppy was walking around making suggestions, but she looked unhappy, too.

"Jack Frost has ruined everything!" Libby said, tears in her eyes.

As Kirsty watched the other kids, her eyes fell on someone she hadn't noticed before. On the farthest corner of one of the picnic blankets, separated from everyone else, sat a boy in a floppy sunhat. He had a notebook on his lap and was bent over it, scribbling as fast as he could. As Kirsty watched, he paused, read what he'd written, and chuckled gleefully to himself. Then he went back to scribbling.

"Rachel, look at that boy sitting over there by himself," Kirsty whispered. "He seems to have *tons* of ideas. He can't stop writing!"

Rachel glanced at the boy. At the same moment, he happened to look up for a second, and Rachel spotted a long, green nose under the brim of his hat.

"That's not a boy," she said to Kirsty and Libby. "He's a goblin!"

"What should we do?" Kirsty asked anxiously.

But before they could say anything else, Poppy also spotted the goblin writing away. Her face lit up, and she hurried over to him.

"You seem to have a lot of ideas!"

Poppy said with a smile. "How much have you written?"

"Pages and pages!" the goblin said proudly, flipping through his notebook. Rachel, Kirsty, and Libby could see that he'd already filled almost half of it.

"Would you read your story to us?" Poppy asked. "We'd all love to hear it."

"It's not finished yet," the goblin mumbled.

"That doesn't matter," Poppy assured him. "Don't be shy! Stand up, and let's hear it. What's your story called?"

"It's called *The Greatest Goblin Who Ever Lived!*" the goblin replied proudly. He climbed to his feet, cleared his throat, and held the notebook up. As he did, Libby let out a horrified gasp.

"I see why that goblin is such a good

writer," she declared indignantly to Rachel and Kirsty. "It's because he has my magic notebook! We have to get it away from him—but I don't know how!"

Thrilling Tale

Kirsty and Rachel looked more closely at the goblin's notebook. They could see it glowing faintly with a golden haze of magic!

"Once upon a time," the goblin read, "Jack Frost lived in a castle made of ice in the middle of a dark, snowy land. Jack Frost was grumpy and selfish,

and all he did was order his goblins
around and make them do what he said.

"'Do this!' Jack Frost yelled. 'Do that!
And hurry up!'

"The goblins always tried their best,
but Jack Frost was never satisfied.

"'You fools!' he would roar furiously,
shooting bolts of ice at them from his
magic wand. 'I'm fed up with all of you!'

"The goblins would scurry around and
try even harder to do exactly what Jack
Frost wanted, but he was never happy.

"So at last, one brave goblin decided to
stand up for himself. . . ."

As the goblin read, Rachel, Kirsty, and
Libby exchanged amused glances.
According to the author, the goblin in
the story was smarter, braver, and more
handsome than any other goblin, ever. It

was obvious that the goblin was writing about himself! However, when the goblin described how his hero got the better of Jack Frost, pelting him with a flurry of huge snowballs until Jack Frost begged for mercy, everyone in the audience was spellbound—even Libby and the girls. The story was thrilling!

"And so the handsome, brave, smart goblin became Emperor of the Ice Castle," the goblin declared. "And he ruled over Jack Frost and the other goblins wisely and well. But behind the scenes, Jack Frost was plotting and planning dark deeds! He was determined to regain his Ice Throne and rule the kingdom once again. . . ."

The goblin stopped reading, and everyone broke into applause.

"That was wonderful!" Poppy gasped. "So imaginative!"

"Tell us what happens next," begged a girl, but the goblin shook his head.

"I haven't finished the story yet," he said, and the audience groaned with disappointment.

"The goblin's story is a big hit," Libby whispered to Rachel and Kirsty. "But it's my magic notebook that turned him into such a wonderful author!"

"Can't you write the rest of it now?" Poppy asked the goblin. "Everyone is eager to hear what Jack Frost does next. He's a wonderful character—a real bad guy!"

"You're lucky that Jack Frost isn't

here!" another boy called. He was sitting in the back of the group, wearing a bright green hat. "Otherwise you'd be in *big* trouble!"

Rachel could see that the goblin looked nervous when he heard that.

"We'll take a break to have some juice and cookies," Poppy announced, smiling at the goblin. "That will give you time to write more of your fantastic story!"

"Maybe we should try and get the notebook back now," Kirsty suggested quietly to Rachel and Libby. "I thought of a plan that might work."

"Yes, go for it!" Libby agreed eagerly. She tucked herself inside Rachel's pencil case, and the girls walked over to the goblin. He was sitting on the picnic blanket again, getting ready to write another chapter.

"Your story really is amazing!" Kirsty told him.

"I know," the goblin said happily, puffing out his chest.

"We'd really like to read it again,"
Kirsty went on. "Would you swap
notebooks with me for a minute? You
can read my story about a squirrel, even
though it's not half as good as yours."

The goblin studied them suspiciously.
Then he squealed with rage. "I can see
that fairy hiding in your pencil case!" he
hissed at Rachel. "Leave me alone!"
Clutching the notebook tightly to his
chest, he jumped up and
raced away.

"Sorry, girls, he
saw me peeking
out!" Libby said
with a gasp.

"Don't worry,
Libby," Rachel
assured her. "We'll

catch him!" She and Kirsty ran off after the goblin.

Some of the other kids noticed the goblin running away, and they followed, shouting, "Come back! We want to hear the rest of your story!"

The goblin bolted across the playground, dodging the swings and the sandbox. Then, to the girls' dismay, he seemed to vanish! But Rachel spotted him climbing up a tree in the distance, just before he disappeared into the highest branches. Quickly, Libby and the girls ran after him.

"Where did that boy go?" asked one of the other kids. Everyone looked very disappointed when they couldn't spot the goblin anywhere. After a few minutes, they all gave up and headed back to the

workshop. Meanwhile, Kirsty and
Rachel slipped behind the tree, out of
sight.

"Fairies can't climb, but they can fly!"
Libby whispered, smiling. With one
swish of her wand, Rachel and Kirsty
were instantly transformed into tiny,
winged fairies! Together, the three
friends all flew up into the tree.

The goblin was sitting on a branch, still gripping the notebook. He yelped in angry surprise when Libby and the girls appeared. He began edging warily along the branch, away from them.

"Go away!" the goblin roared.

"Let's try and get the notebook," Libby whispered to the girls. "We'll just have to be careful the goblin doesn't fall out of the tree!"

The three of them took turns swooping
down, trying to grab the notebook, but
the goblin kept swatting them away with
his free hand. Then Kirsty had an idea!
Instead of flying down from above, she
flew *underneath* the branch — and popped
up right in front of the goblin.

"*Aaargh!*" he screamed, throwing up
his hands in fright. He dropped
the magic notebook!
Rachel and Libby
raced to catch it, but
they were just a
second too late.
The notebook
tumbled down
through the air.

Suddenly, the boy in
the green hat from the

43

workshop appeared under the tree. He caught the notebook and glanced up to see where it had come from. Kirsty's heart sank as she saw a long, green nose underneath the hat.

"It's another goblin!" she said to her friends with a frown. "And he has the magic notebook!"

How would they ever get the notebook back now?

Success
Story

"Now it's *my* turn to write a story in the
magic notebook!" the goblin cried in
glee. Waving the notebook over his head,
he skipped off toward the playground.
Libby, Rachel, and Kirsty all groaned.

"After him, girls!" Libby yelled.
Leaving the other goblin to climb down
the tree, the three fairy friends zoomed
off.

When Libby, Rachel, and Kirsty
caught up with the goblin in the green
hat, they found him perched on the
jungle gym. He was
scribbling frantically in
the magic notebook,
muttering the words
aloud to himself.

"'The goblin in
the green hat
raced up to the
battlements of the
Ice Castle, where
he found the goblin
emperor waiting for him.'

"'Now we'll see who's the most
handsome, smart, and brave goblin of
them all!' the goblin in the hat cried."

As the goblin continued his story,

describing how the two goblins fought an exciting duel, some of the other kids from the writing workshop hurried over to listen.

"We'll have to wait until everyone's gone before we try to get the notebook again," Libby whispered, waving for the girls to hide behind one of the slides.

Rachel nodded. But she couldn't help noticing how entranced the audience was with the goblin's story. Suddenly, an idea popped into her head! She quickly whispered it to Kirsty and Libby:

"You want me to disguise you as Crafts Week judges?" Libby raised her eyebrows. "Of course I can do that!"

Libby waved her wand over Kirsty and Rachel, and glittery fairy sparkles fell softly around them. When the magic mist cleared, the girls looked at each other in surprise. Kirsty wore a pair of glasses and her hair was pulled back in a ponytail, while Rachel wore a big sunhat with the brim pulled down low. Both girls were wearing pretty floral dresses instead of their T-shirts and shorts.

"Good luck!" Libby whispered, sliding into the pocket of Kirsty's dress with a wink. Then the girls hurried out from behind the slide.

The goblin was just finishing his story. "And the goblin in the baseball hat became the new Emperor of the Ice Castle!" he cried. "His powerful magic changed his baseball hat into a golden crown, glimmering with sparkling green emeralds. . . ."

As the kids all applauded, Kirsty and Rachel walked up to the goblin.

"Your story was wonderful!" Kirsty told him. "My friend and I are Crafts Week judges. Your story is so good, we want everyone, everywhere, to read it!"

"Hooray!" the goblin cheered, waving the magic notebook around his head in excitement.

"We want to turn your story into a book that will be in every bookstore and library in the world," Rachel said as the other kids began to drift back to the workshop.

"To do that, we'll need your notebook," Kirsty added, holding out her hand. She tried not to look too eager. Would the goblin agree—or would he guess what they were up to?

Happy Ending

"Sure!" the goblin agreed immediately, handing the magic notebook to Kirsty. Both girls breathed huge sighs of relief as Libby zoomed out of Kirsty's pocket.

"Give that back, you pesky fairy!" the goblin screeched furiously as Libby took her precious notebook. As the notebook shrank to its Fairyland size in a cloud of sparkling magic, the goblin who'd been in the tree ran over to the jungle gym.

"You lost the notebook, you fool!" he yelled, glaring at the other goblin.

"Don't call me a fool!" the second goblin shouted. "My story was a million times more exciting than yours!"

Libby winked at the girls and quickly waved her wand. There was a burst of sparkling fairy dust. Suddenly, both goblins looked surprised to find themselves holding a book bound in bright green leather with gold writing on the cover.

"Now you each have a copy of your own story," Libby said with a smile.

The goblins looked thrilled.

"I'll read you my story," the first goblin said as they headed off across the park.

"No, I'll read you *my* story!" the other goblin snapped back.

As the goblins wandered into the distance, still arguing, Libby turned to

Rachel and Kirsty. "Girls, our story today will have a very happy ending, thanks to you!" She smiled. "I can't tell you how grateful I am. Your friendship and loyalty mean so much to all of us in Fairyland." Then, with one flick of her wand, Libby's magic swept away the girls' disguises, returning them to normal. "Now go and enjoy the rest of your writing workshop," Libby said. "I'll see you very soon!" With a wave, she vanished.

When Kirsty and Rachel rejoined the workshop, they could already see a difference. All the kids were writing in their notebooks,

brows furrowed in concentration. Poppy
was also looking much happier as she
walked around, offering advice.

"I feel like I'm bursting with ideas
now!" Kirsty remarked, flipping open

her notebook. "I thought of a fantastic
adventure for my squirrel."

"I'm going to finish the story about the
Rainbow Fairies we started earlier,"
Rachel decided. "I can remember
everything that happened now!"

The girls began to write, and soon they
were absorbed in their stories. They
scribbled away, occasionally
stopping to read
different parts out
loud to each other.

"You're working
hard!" Poppy
commented,
walking over.

"Can I see what you've written?"

Feeling shy, Rachel handed over her
notebook.

"Rachel, this story is wonderfully creative!" Poppy declared with a smile. "I love your seven fairy characters, especially Ruby the Red Fairy. You've made them so real, they could almost fly off the page!"

"Thank you, Poppy," Rachel said proudly.

"I think you should enter this in the Crafts Week competition," Poppy went on, handing the notebook back to Rachel.

"That's perfect, Rachel!" Kirsty exclaimed happily. "Now we'll *both* have an entry in the competition tomorrow."

Just then, Poppy clapped her hands to get everyone's attention. "I'm afraid the workshop is over," she announced. "I hope you all enjoyed it. And to end the day, I have some signed copies of my latest book for you. It's called *A Rainspell Island Fairy Tale*."

Kirsty and Rachel grinned at each other. The new book sounded fabulous. They couldn't wait to read it! But they couldn't help feeling awfully lucky. After all, even Poppy Fields, the famous author, didn't know about their secret fairy friends! Rachel and Kirsty couldn't wait for their next fairy adventure!

THE MAGICAL CRAFTS FAIRIES

Rachel and Kirsty have found Kayla,
Annabelle, Zadie, Josie, Violet, and Libby's
missing magic objects. Now it's time for
them to help the final Magical
Crafts Fairy

Join their next adventure
in this special sneak peek. . . .

Exhibition Day

"I'm so sad that it's our last day of vacation," Kirsty Tate sighed, placing a pile of folded T-shirts in her suitcase. "But I'm super excited about the Crafts Week exhibition and competition today!"

"So am I," Rachel Walker agreed. The girls were in Kirsty's attic bedroom at the b and b, getting their things ready to head home that evening. They'd spent the week on Rainspell Island, staying every other night at the b and b with Mr. and Mrs. Tate, and alternate nights at the campsite with Rachel's parents.

"It's been so much fun trying out all these different crafts, hasn't it?" said Kirsty enthusiastically, and Rachel nodded. It was Crafts Week on Rainspell Island, and for the past six days the girls had attended all sorts of workshops. Today there was an exhibition of the best crafts created during the week. Prizes were going to be awarded!

"And isn't it great that we *both* have entries in the exhibition, Kirsty?" Rachel asked, stuffing socks into her suitcase. "I think your painting of me under a rainbow should definitely win a prize."

"No, I think your story about us meeting the Rainbow Fairies on our first visit to Rainspell Island should win!" Kirsty laughed. "Of course, no one except us knows that it's all true!"

At that moment, Mrs. Tate came in. "Girls, have you finished packing yet?" she asked.

"Almost, Mom," Kirsty replied, putting her bathroom bag into her suitcase. "Can we bring our entries to Artie for the exhibition now?" Artie Johnson was the organizer of the Rainspell Island Crafts Week.

"Then we agreed to help bake cakes and cookies to serve at the exhibition this afternoon," Rachel added.

"I'm looking forward to tasting them!" Mrs. Tate said with a smile. "Off you go! We'll see you at the exhibition later."

The girls called good-bye to Mr. Tate and hurried out of the b and b. Rachel carried the notebook that author Poppy Fields had given her at the writing workshop, and Kirsty had her painting tucked under her arm.

A huge tent had been set up on the boardwalk for the exhibition. The girls slipped inside and quickly found Artie and her helpers setting up tables.

"Hello, girls," Artie said, beaming at them. "Do you have something for me?"

Rachel and Kirsty handed over the notebook and painting.

"Good luck in the competition," Artie told them. "What are you doing until then?"

"We're going to the Sunshine Cake

Shop," Rachel explained. "We're helping bake goodies for the exhibition."

"My husband, Ben, is the head baker there," Artie said, her eyes twinkling. "I'm sure he'll be delighted to have some extra hands helping out!"

After saying good-bye to Artie, the girls left the tent and walked back along the boardwalk to Main Street.

"The exhibition is going to be so much fun!" Rachel said excitedly.

"As long as Jack Frost doesn't ruin everything," Kirsty replied with a sigh.

RAINBOW magic™

Which Magical Fairies Have You Met?

- ❑ The Rainbow Fairies
- ❑ The Weather Fairies
- ❑ The Jewel Fairies
- ❑ The Pet Fairies
- ❑ The Dance Fairies
- ❑ The Music Fairies
- ❑ The Sports Fairies
- ❑ The Party Fairies
- ❑ The Ocean Fairies
- ❑ The Night Fairies
- ❑ The Magical Animal Fairies
- ❑ The Princess Fairies
- ❑ The Superstar Fairies
- ❑ The Fashion Fairies
- ❑ The Sugar & Spice Fairies
- ❑ The Earth Fairies

📖 SCHOLASTIC

Find all of your favorite fairy friends at
scholastic.com/rainbowmagic

HiT entertainment

RMFAIRY